Rain Romp

stomping away a grouchy day

by Jane Kurtz
pictures by Dyanna Wolcott

GREENWILLOW BOOKS *An Imprint of* HarperCollins*Publishers*

Gray day.
Gray, grouchy day.
Mom tugs my toes.
"Rise and shine," she says.
I won't get up.
I don't feel shiny.

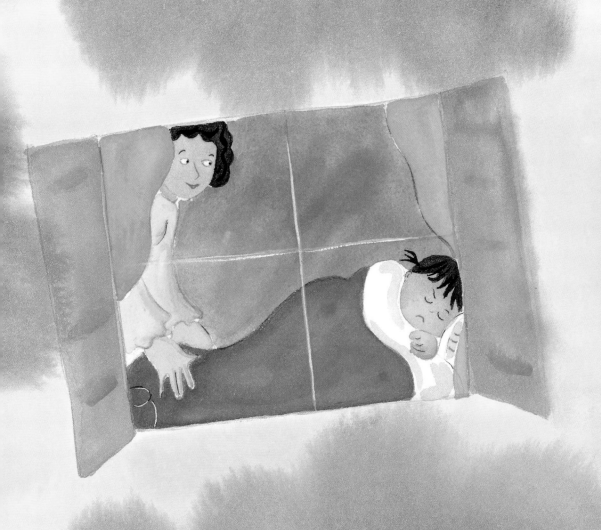

The sky
agrees with me.

Dad hums a snazzy, jazzy tune.

"Ohhh, it's nice to get up in the morning," he croons.

"No way," I say. "Nooooo way."

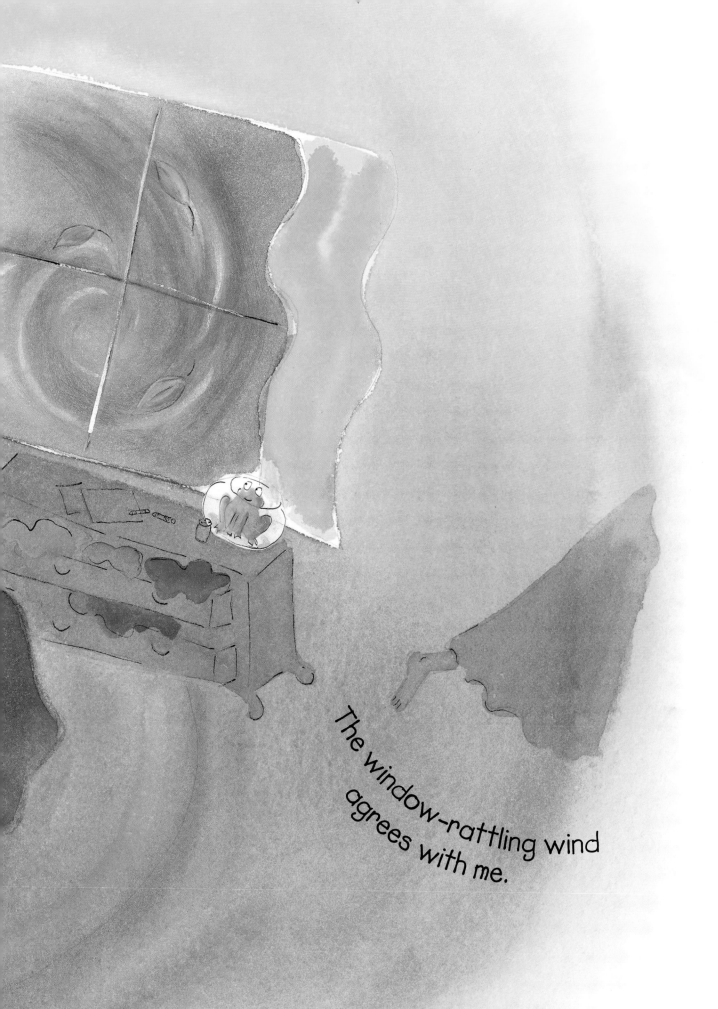

The window-rattling wind
agrees with me.

Mom and Dad waltz up and down.
Dad yodels.
Mom laughs.
I snarl and frown.
A drizzle starts dripping
a long, sad song.

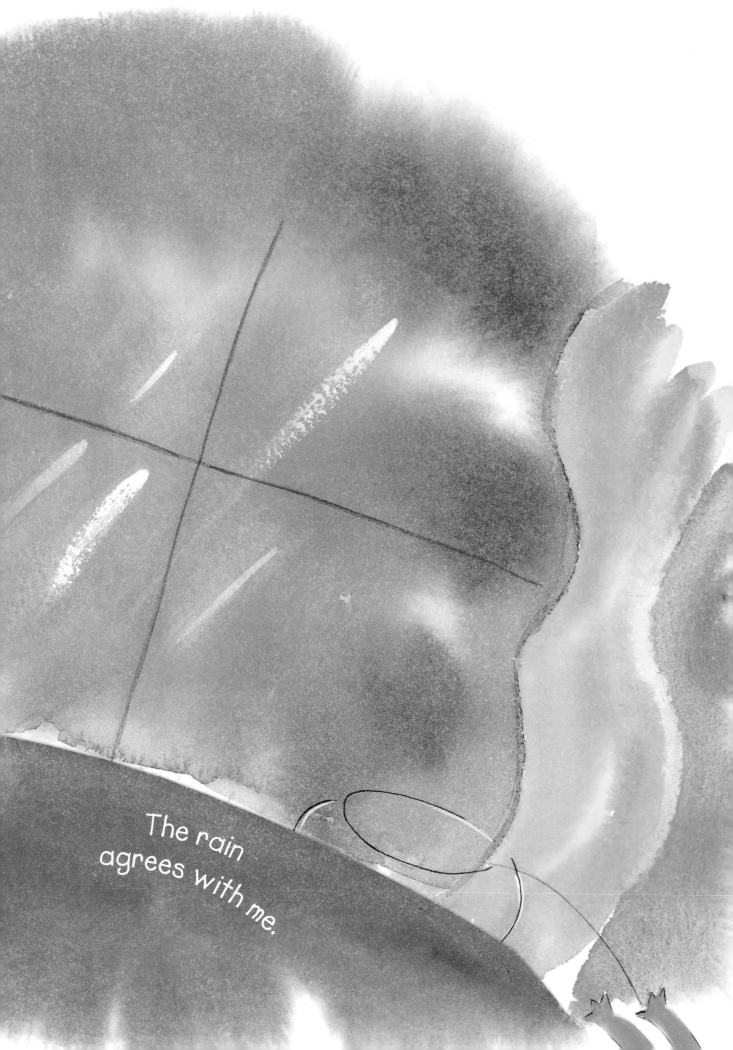

The rain
agrees with me.

"Mad as a wet hen," Mom says.

"You know it!" says Dad, and off they go.

Wet hen?
Pooh!

The sky and I
are two

howling
prowling
scowling
wolverines.

I leap out of bed,

knock over my chairs,

rush down the stairs,

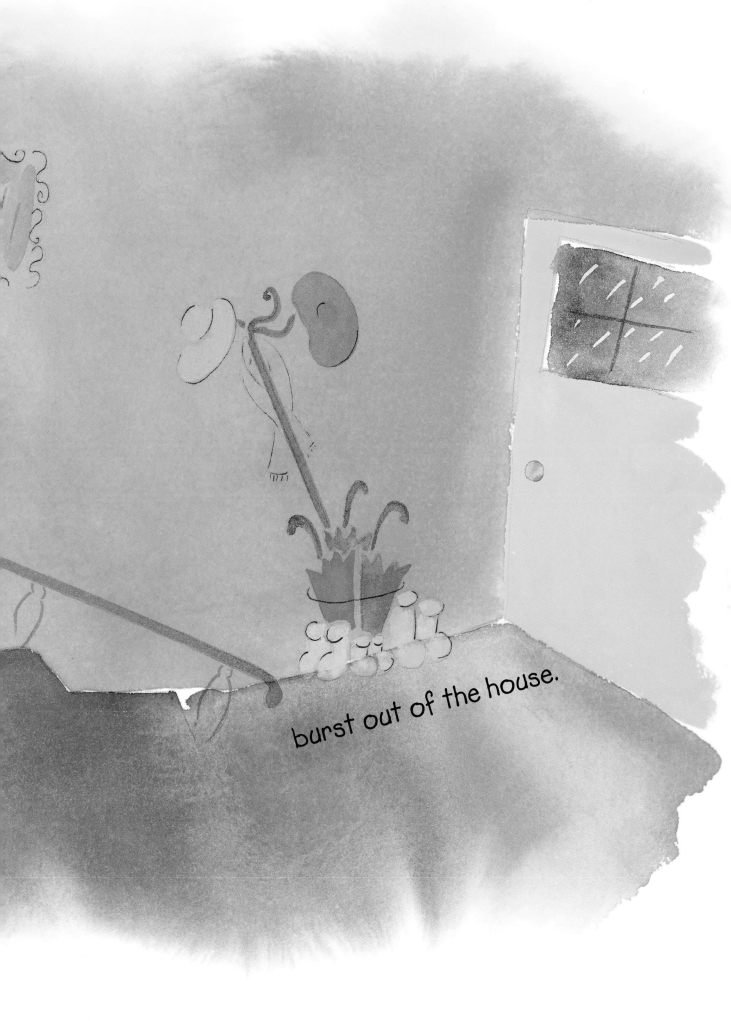

burst out of the house.

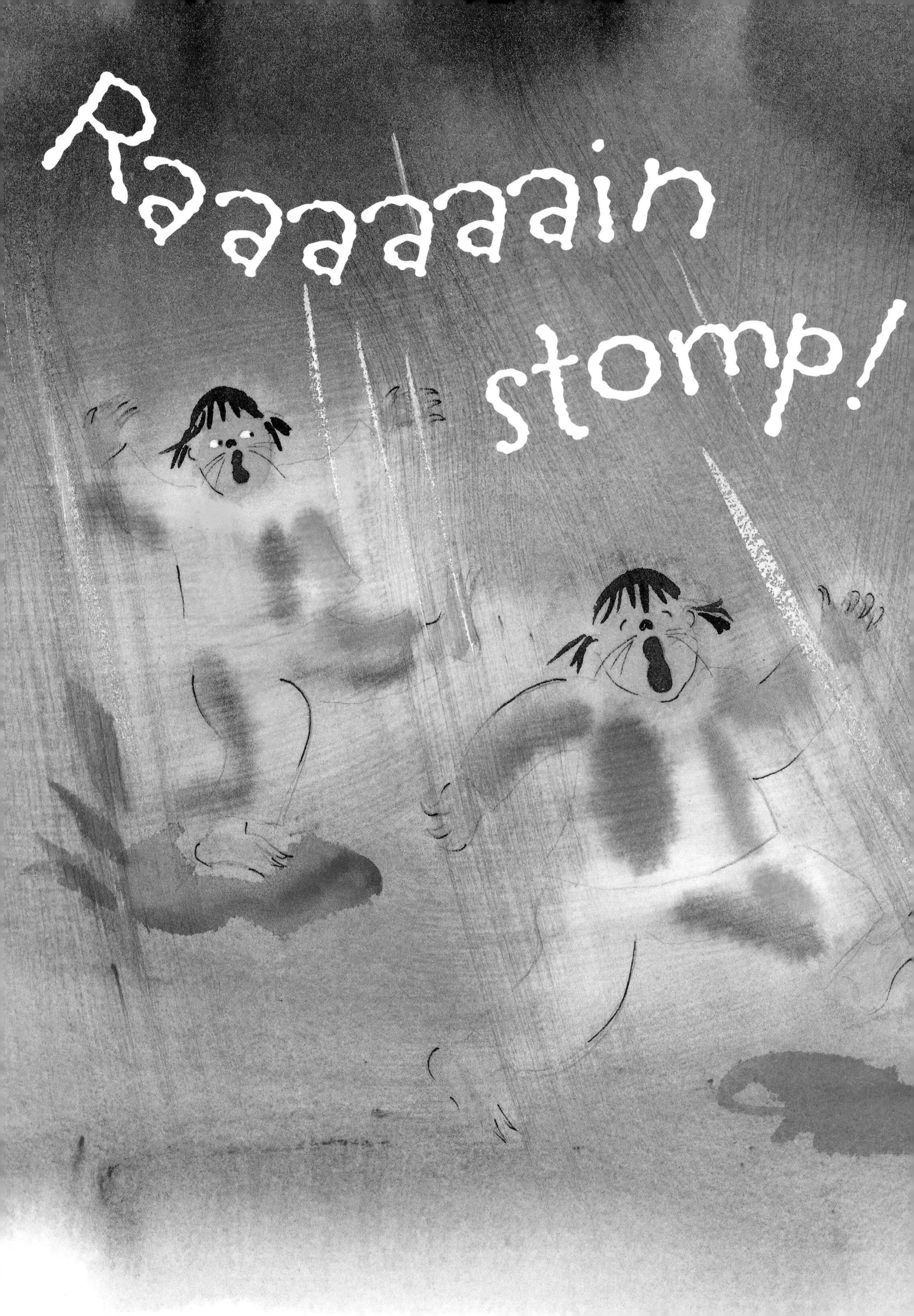
Raaaaaain
stomp!

Mom's and Dad's faces
bob in the window like two balloons.

Scolding

frowning

puzzling

smiling

laughing.

romp!

We dance in whooshing, swooshing leaves.

The thunder rumbles, shaking our bones.

Little silver worms of rain

wriggle and slither under our shirts.

The whole world smells like dark, wet dir

I stretch out my hands to Dad and Mom.
The grouchiness is almost gone.

And gradually the storm is, too.
The thunder quits grumbling.
The wind fizzles.
The rain drizzles,
drips,
stops.

The wolverines have wandered off.
The sky and I are soft gray moths.
"I want to go inside," I say.
I wave the sky good-bye.

Dad builds a fire that cracks and clicks,
nibbles the middles out of sticks.
We hold our fingers to the strands.
The warmth leaps out and licks our hands.
Dad yodels.
Mom laughs.
I start to sing.

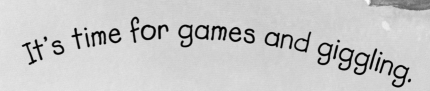

It's time for games and giggling.

When I'm cold, and when I'm hot,
when I'm cheerful, when I'm not—
the three of us will always be
an all-weather,
stick-together,
stomp-it-out,
romp-it-out,
love-you, hug-you family.